F
Par   Park, Barbara
        The Kid in the red
        jacket

DATE DUE			
5-8			
11-18			
9-17			

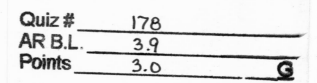

Quiz #   178
AR B.L.   3.9
Points   3.0   G

92   88

MEDIALOG
Alexandria, Ky 41001

The Kid
in the
Red Jacket

ALSO BY BARBARA PARK

Don't Make Me Smile
Operation: Dump the Chump
Skinnybones
Beanpole
Buddies

The Kid
in the
Red Jacket

by
Barbara Park

Alfred A. Knopf, New York

This is a Borzoi Book published by Alfred A. Knopf, Inc.

Copyright © 1987 by Barbara Park
Cover illustration copyright © 1987 by Rob Sauber
All rights reserved under International and Pan-American Copyright Conventions. Published in the United States by Alfred A. Knopf, Inc., New York, and simultaneously in Canada by Random House of Canada Limited, Toronto. Distributed by Random House, Inc., New York. Manufactured in the United States of America

3 5 7 9 0 8 6 4 2

Library of Congress Cataloging-in-Publication Data
Park, Barbara. The kid in the red jacket.
Summary: When ten-year-old Howard has to move with his family to a distant state, he is forced to live on a street named Chester Pewe, adjust to a new school, and get used to being shadowed by the little girl in a nearby house. [1. Moving, Household—Fiction. 2. Humorous stories] I. Title. PZ7.P2197Ki 1987
[Fic] 86-20113
ISBN 0-394-88189-3   ISBN 0-394-98189-8 (lib. bdg.)

This one's for Sibyl
(who could
definitely write a book of her own!)

The Kid
in the
Red Jacket

1

"My leg's hot," I announced as our car pulled out of our driveway.

It was the day of the "big move." At least that's what my parents kept calling it. I hated that. It's not that I didn't realize moving from Arizona to Massachusetts was "big." It's just that when they said it, they made it seem real exciting and fun. They never made it sound like what it really was—rotten.

My mother turned around and gave me one of

her looks. "Please, Howard, don't start. We haven't even made it to the street yet."

I glanced over at my baby brother, Gaylord. He was sitting happily in his car seat, staring at his hands. He had just discovered his hands, and he kept opening and closing them like they were some great new invention.

I reached out and touched his leg.

"Gaylord's leg isn't hot," I reported. "Gaylord's in the shade. Has anyone ever noticed how Gaylord always gets the shade? I mean, I'm aware that he's a baby and everything, but I don't think you should play favorites like this. I think we should flip a coin for the shady side."

When no one said anything, I leaned toward him. "What's that, Gaylord?" I asked. "You want what?"

I tapped my father on the shoulder. "Gaylord says he wants to switch places. He says he wants to get some sun on those lily-white legs of his."

My mother just sighed. She probably would have yelled, but I had been making her yell so much lately, I think she was getting sort of sick of it. Normally, parents really enjoy yelling. But I guess it's like anything else—too much of a good thing, and it's not as fun anymore.

What's weird is, until this move came along, I hardly made my parents yell at all. I don't mean I am an angel or anything. But I get good grades at school, and I've never been arrested. I don't think parents can ask for much more than that.

I used to actually even *like* my parents. They had always been pretty understanding, pretty fair. They didn't go around tickling me in public or embarrassing me the way some parents do. That's what was so crazy about our "big move." They hardly even discussed it with me! I'm not kidding. My father just came home all excited one day and told me he'd gotten this big promotion and we'd be moving to Massachusetts. That was it! We didn't even take a vote!

He made it sound real cheery, of course. Whenever parents announce something you're going to hate, they try to spice it up and make it sound better than it is. They kept calling the move "a great new adventure." Then they spent a lot of time telling me how much better off I was going to be because of my father's new job. They talked about college and my future, stuff I couldn't care less about right now. So instead of feeling better, mostly I just felt sick to my stomach.

I cried a lot after I found out. I didn't do it much in front of my parents, though. When you're ten and a half, you don't like a lot of people sitting around watching your nose run. That's why I saved most of it for my room, muffling my blubbering sounds with my pillow. Sometimes it got so soggy, I couldn't sleep on it.

I was also more scared than I'd ever been before. But it wasn't the kind of scared you feel when you think there's a dead guy with a hatchet hiding in your closet at night. It was a new kind of scared. Moving makes you feel all alone inside. You don't know what the new town is going to look like, or your new house, or your street, or even what kind of people you'll meet. It may not *sound* scary. But if you ever have to move, you'll understand what I mean.

Anyway, besides making me feel sad and scared, the whole idea of moving also made me furious. How could my parents do this to me? How could they just whisk me away from all my friends, and my school, and my soccer team, and then tell me what a "great new adventure" I was going to have? Did they actually expect me to be happy about it? Did they think that I had no feelings? That they could just pick me up like some dumb stuffed animal and set me down any old place, and I'd be fine?

As the car neared the end of my street, I started fidgeting.

"I'm bored and my leg's hot," I whined. "Also, I think I might be getting carsick."

At the wheel, I saw my father shaking his head in disgust. "Come on, Howard. Not today, okay? Why don't you take some time off from complaining and just relax?"

Relax? I thought to myself. *Are you kidding? Complaining is my job now. It's what I do.*

Suddenly my mother reached into a bag in the front seat and tossed me back an orange. She does this sort of thing a lot when we're traveling. Since I've never been what you'd call a good little traveler, my mother buys a bunch of stuff to keep me busy so I won't gripe. When you think about it, it's kind of insulting—like feeding a gorilla a bunch of bananas so he won't bother you.

I was particularly annoyed at my mother lately—especially after what I heard her say to Aunt Emily on the phone. It happened a couple of days before we moved. I was sitting on the back stairs, so she didn't know I was around.

"Yeah, he's not too happy about it right now,

Em," she had said. "But you know how kids are. Once you get them there, they always seem to bounce right back."

Bounce right back! I'm not kidding. She really said that! She made me sound like a Nerf ball. Like she had a foam rubber son with no emotions at all!

The more I thought about it, the more annoyed I got. I tried to take my mind off things by looking out the window, but my father's voice distracted me.

"Hmm," he said, pondering out loud. "I wonder if the van will get to Massachusetts before we do."

The moving van! Why did he have to bring up that stupid moving van? I hated that van and all the stupid moving men that came with it! The day they packed our stuff had been the worst day of my life.

My parents were upstairs when the knock came at the door. "Answer that, would you, Howard?" called my father. "We're busy up here."

"I can't!" I called back. "I'm in my pajamas!"

My father was standing at the top of the stairs with his hands full. "No one cares what you're wearing, Howard. Just let the men inside."

"*I* care what I'm wearing! Have you seen these

things? Would someone please tell Nana that I'm too old for Porky Pig pajamas?"

"Howard!"

My father was using his killing voice. You can push him so far, but when he uses his killing voice, it's best to do what he says. I went to the door.

"Hi, sonny."

There were three of them, all lined up in their brown moving-men suits. They came inside. One of them looked at my pajamas and whistled. "Porky Pig, eh?" he asked.

I covered Porky with my hands and ran up to my room. Then I locked the door so no one could come in. Later, when the movers were ready to pack my stuff, my father got a key and opened it.

It still makes me sick when I think about it. The moving man stomped right in and started dumping all my stuff into big boxes. He just heaped it together like it was garbage or something. When the marbles fell out of my Chinese checkers, he dumped them in the box without even putting them back in the game first. It really made me furious. I don't even *like* Chinese checkers, but a guy still likes to keep his marbles together. . . .

I concentrated harder on looking out the car window. As luck would have it, we were just passing Thornsberry's house. Seeing it gave me this real empty feeling in the pit of my stomach. Barry Thornsberry is one of my best friends. Saying good-bye to him and to my other best friend, Roger Grimsley, had been the hardest thing I'd ever had to do in my whole life. The three of us practically grew up together. I know this sounds mean, but I felt closer to Thornsberry and Roger than I did to my very own baby brother. I mean, we've even known each other longer—since preschool. Our teacher, Miss Filbert, introduced us and assigned us to the same work table.

Thornsberry was crying at the time. Of the three of us, he's the most sensitive. He thought his mother had given him to Miss Filbert for keeps. It took him about a week to figure things out.

I didn't like Thornsberry at first. It's hard to get to know a kid who only talks to you from behind a Kleenex. I liked Roger, though. On the first day of school, Miss Filbert asked us to draw a picture of our family. Roger drew a cow.

"Uh, that's a very nice cow, Roger," she said. "But are you sure you understood the project? You were supposed to draw a picture of your family."

Roger just smiled happily and nodded.

Later we learned that cows were the only things Roger could draw. By the end of the year, Miss Filbert had taught him to stand them on two legs and dress them in clothes. Personally, I thought this was a big mistake. In kindergarten, every time Roger drew a picture of his family, it looked like they all had cow heads.

Before the move, I'd talked a lot of my worries over with Thornsberry and Roger. They hated my leaving almost as much as I did, but they tried to make me feel better about it.

"Come on, Howard," said Thornsberry. "Maybe it won't be as bad as you think."

"How could it not be bad?" I asked glumly. "Didn't you ever study about Massachusetts in history? The Pilgrims moved there, and by the first winter practically all of them were dead."

Roger made a face. "I hate Pilgrims. I've hated them ever since my mother made me be one on Halloween. Remember that? She made me wear that stupid top hat and long black coat. Everyone thought I was Abraham Lincoln carrying a turkey."

Thornsberry gave me a funny look. "You don't really think you're going to *die* there, do you, Howard?"

"Well, maybe not actually *die*," I admitted. "But I'm going to have to go to a stupid new school, and that's almost like dying."

Every time I thought about it, my stomach tied itself in knots. "God, I can't believe it. I'm actually going to have to be a new kid."

Thornsberry and Roger groaned.

"We got a new kid in our room about a week ago," Roger said. "No one can remember his name, so we just call him by the color of his shirt. On Thursday he was the kid in the green shirt. On Friday he wore a shirt with his name on it, so we called him the kid in the Kenneth shirt."

Thornsberry hit Roger on the arm. "We're supposed to be making him feel better, remember?"

"It doesn't matter," I replied. "It's not like I don't know what happens to new kids. I've had enough of them in my class to see how hard it is to fit in."

"Yeah, but you won't have any trouble, Howard," said Roger. "It's not like you're a geek or anything. At school you're practically even *popular*."

"Sure, Howard," added Roger. "You won't have any trouble. You'll see."

Thinking about how nice they had tried to be

almost made me start to cry. My mother must have heard me sniffle or something, because she turned around.

"What's the matter?" she asked, raising her eyebrows sympathetically.

"Everything," I answered dismally. "Everything's the matter."

She just sighed and turned back around. A second later she threw over a granola bar.

Instead of saying thank you, I made a noise like a gorilla. She didn't say anything, but I'm pretty sure she got the message.

We had turned onto the highway by then, so I spent the next couple of hours reading signs, trying to get my mind off the move. It wasn't easy, though. Every few minutes, we'd pass a billboard with kids painted on it and I'd start wondering about the kids in Massachusetts. What would they be like? Would they dress the same way we did in Arizona? I hoped I would fit in. One time we had a German kid visit our school, and he wore a suit and a bow tie. He looked like a little grandfather or something.

Anyway, all I've got to say is that moving really stunk. And even though it's over now, I still don't blame myself for the way I acted about it. A lot of mean stuff has been done to me—by my parents, by the moving men, and by my father's stupid company. And even though sometimes you can control your anger, you can't control your sadness. And that's what I mostly was, I guess—sad. Sad about leaving my friends and my school and my room and my soccer team and a million other things.

If you've ever been sad, *really* sad, you know what I'm talking about. Sadness is with you all the time. Even when your friends are trying to make you laugh, sadness seems to be waiting right behind your smile.

2

Thanks to Gaylord's screaming, the trip to Massachusetts drove us all crazy. I appreciated the job he did on my parents, but unfortunately I had to listen to him too. For the first two days he was pretty good, but by the time we got to Illinois, Gaylord decided he hated his car seat. He screamed from the minute he was strapped in until he cried himself to sleep. Then when he woke up and found he was still in the car seat, he screamed all over again.

At lunch my mother asked the waitress if she wanted to buy a baby. Everyone went "ha ha," but I really think if the waitress could have come up with the cash, Gaylord would still be on the counter at Denny's.

Anyway, when it came to my brother's crying, my dad wasn't exactly overflowing with patience. Every few minutes he'd turn around and yell, *"For heaven's sake, Gaylord, would you knock it off!"* I'm not kidding. He yelled it about eighty times.

I think we were somewhere outside of Chicago when my father finally cracked. He pulled over to the side of the highway and told Gaylord to get out of the car. For a second my mother and I just sat there looking at my dad like he was nuts. I was pretty relieved when he finally calmed down and started smiling about it.

The only one who didn't seem to be bothered by Gaylord's screaming was my basset hound, Bill. He was sleeping in the back of our station wagon and never even woke up. I guess it's understandable, though. He was on sleeping pills from the vet. Since Bill gets carsick, it was the only way to get him to Massachusetts without making a mess.

Actually the whole thing was pretty interesting.

My mother would slip him one of the sleeping pills in the morning and he would start getting groggy right away. First his legs would go limp, and then he would collapse before we could get him into the car. One morning a little kid was watching in the motel parking lot as my father tried to lift Bill into the car. He started running up and down the sidewalk, screaming, "Doggie dead! Doggie dead!"

I've always liked Bill. My mother says he stinks to high heaven, but it's not because he's dirty. He just has a strong dog odor. Anyone who ever pets him always ends up saying "pew."

It took us five and a half days to finally get to Massachusetts. The town of Rosemont (our new home) was about an hour from the state line. Since it was probably going to be a couple of days before the movers arrived with our stuff, Dad had reserved a motel room.

Mom carried Gaylord inside and put him down on the bed. Right away he started kicking his feet and making baby noises. I think he was showing us how cute he was so no one would kill him for all the crying.

"Keep an eye on your brother for a few minutes,

will you, Howard?" asked Mom. "Dad and I have to run up to the motel office."

You'd think I would have really minded watching such a brat. But even though Gaylord can get on your nerves sometimes, he's probably as good as you can get for a baby. He's all soft and white, of course, but he doesn't seem to be a sissy baby. His infant seat tilted over backward once, and we found him in the living room, quietly standing on his head and looking at the ceiling.

He can actually even be fun once in a while. Like sometimes I'll sit him on my lap and watch his head start bobbing around. Once I told my parents we should have named him Bob. After I said it, I laughed for about two hours. Finally, my father told me to please shut up.

As soon as my parents were gone, I sat down next to Gaylord and looked around us. "Geez, Gaylord, we're really here. I mean it's actually *happening*. We're in a new state, all alone without any friends. . . ."

Gaylord rolled over and tried to grab his stuffed walrus. He has two favorite stuffed animals—Mr. Walrus and Mr. Giraffe. My mother named both of them. Clever, huh? I'm surprised she didn't name Gaylord "Mr. Baby."

Gaylord stuffed part of Mr. Walrus in his mouth and rolled back over.

"No wonder you don't understand how bad this is," I continued. "You got to bring your friends with you. But what about me? What am *I* supposed to do without Roger and Thornsberry?"

Gaylord made a squeaking sound.

"Oh, sure, I know I've got *you*. But let's face facts, little fella, you're two feet tall and you don't understand English. No offense, but right now you're more like a pet."

My mother surprised me by opening the door. "You two having a nice little chat?" she asked cheerfully.

Quickly I jumped up from the bed. I hate it when she sneaks up on me like that. If I'm not careful, she'll catch me doing something nice and think I'm "bouncing back."

Just then the phone rang. It was the moving company.

"You're kidding! That's terrific!" my father exclaimed after a few seconds. "You mean they'll actually be ready to unload tomorrow? Those drivers really must have put the pedal to the metal!"

I hate it when Dad tries to talk like a truckdriver. It never sounds natural. His handle on our

CB radio is Big Jake. The stupid part is, my father's name is Clifford. Every time he says "Big Jake," my mother falls over on the seat laughing. Once she was laughing so hard, my father had to turn the CB off so no truckers would hear.

After a few more calls to the electric company and the phone company, Dad took us over to the new house to make sure everything was ready. I didn't want to go. I begged and begged to stay at the motel, but they wouldn't let me.

I'm not sure why I hated going so much, but I'd been dreading it for a long time. I'd barely even looked at the pictures of it my parents had tried to show me. See, to me my old house wasn't just a building. It was part of my family, kind of like my dog. And to stand around oohing and aahing over pictures of the new one would have been pretty heartless, if you ask me. It's something a traitor would do.

I was right about the new house too. I knew it as soon as we pulled into the driveway. It didn't look like part of our family at all! It was big and old and looked nothing like my Arizona house. It was made out of brick and was two stories tall. It had this giant porch that went almost the whole way around. You see houses like it on TV a lot.

There are usually a couple of people sitting outside in rocking chairs, talking about good old-fashioned lemonade.

Next to the front door was a plaque that read BUILT 1768. When my mother saw it, she practically went nuts.

"Wow, Howard, look at that! 1768! This house is part of the history of our country! This'll certainly be something to write Roger and Thorny about, won't it?"

I sighed. I could just see the letter now:

Dear Roger and Thornsberry,

My new house is part of the history of our country . . .

Whoopee.

As soon as we were all inside, my father came up and patted me on the back. "This house is over two hundred years old, son. Maybe George Washington even slept here."

If that was supposed to impress me, it didn't. As a matter of fact, the thought of a dead president sleeping in my room sort of made me sick.

After that, my father took me on a tour of the house. In practically every room, he'd stop and tell me to take a look at how much bigger it was than our old house. He was right, too. The rooms were gigantic. The whole thing sort of reminded me of a museum. *Tyrannosaurus rex* could watch TV in our living room and not even feel cramped.

But big doesn't always mean better. Take my room, for instance. Just because it was big, my father tried to make it seem like the answer to a kid's dreams or something. The school cafeteria's big, but I wouldn't want to sleep there.

"Can you believe the space in here, Howard?" Dad went on. "It's at least twice the size of your old bedroom. Maybe even three times! You and your friends can really have some breathing room up here!"

"I don't *have* any friends, Dad," I replied smugly. "When you don't have any friends, they don't breathe that much."

My father put his arm around me and squeezed gently. "You'll make friends, son. You'll make them. Meanwhile, why don't you just give this place a chance, okay? Why don't you stand here at the window and get to know the neighborhood while Mom and I check out the bathrooms."

After he left, I sauntered over to the window and looked out. A huge oak tree stood nearby, and its branches practically touched the windowpane. Looking through them, I could see almost every house on my block. They were all huge. And they all looked every bit as old as mine did. Some were brick and some were painted white with green or black shutters. The house on the corner was painted gray and dark red. It reminded me of a gigantic, old-fashioned dollhouse.

Near the gray house was a street sign. It was pretty far away, and the letters were just a blur. Squinting at it, I realized that for the first time in my life, I didn't even know what street I lived on. This probably wouldn't have worried a lot of kids, but it worried me. If you get lost and you don't know the name of your street, you can end up living at the bus station, wearing plastic bags.

I strained my eyes until I brought the letters into focus.

"Hmmm, let's see. C-H-E-S-T-E-R-P-E-W-E." I looked hard, but no more letters came into view.

Quickly I ran to the doorway. "Hey, Dad, what's the name of our street? I can see the letters, but I can't pronounce it!" I shouted.

From somewhere down the hall came his answer. *"Chester Pewe!"*

For a minute I just stood there, letting it slowly

sink in. After that, I panicked.

"Chester Pewe?" I shouted. "Are you kidding me? I'm living on a street named *Chester Pewe?* Does anyone know how humiliating this is going to be? What kind of idiot would name a street *Chester Pewe?"*

My mother stuck her head out a doorway. "It's a name, Howard! He was probably one of the town's founding fathers. Maybe even a Revolutionary War hero!"

Oh, that makes it a lot better, I thought angrily. Some old pewie soldier names a street after himself, and now *I* have to live on it.

"Do you know what this is going to do to my future?" I shouted back down the hall. "I'll never be able to write to Thornsberry or Roger or anyone! I'll be too embarrassed to include my return address. And don't think they wouldn't laugh at it, either. They'd probably fall right over on the floor and never be able to get up."

This time no one responded. But knowing they were trying to ignore me only made me yell louder.

"Well, so much for me ever getting a pen pal! I really wanted a pen pal too! I was thinking about writing to some kids in Egypt after I got settled."

I don't know why I said that. It just sort of popped into my head. It didn't matter, though. No one was listening anyway.

I sighed and stationed myself back at the window. That's when I saw her. A little girl was just coming out of the brick house across the street. She was wearing a fireman's hat. I figured that made her around six years old. After six, you usually have too much pride to wear a fireman's hat out in public.

I could tell right away the girl was weird. The first thing she did was to grab the garden hose and drag it out to the sidewalk. Then she stood there and pretended to squirt stuff. The water wasn't on, but she held the hose with two hands and pretended it was as hard to control as a real fire hose.

A man walked by and she pretended to squirt him in the back. He turned around and said something to her, and she put the hose down. As soon as he turned the corner, she picked it right up again.

I guess by this time she was tired of pretending. That's when she turned on the hose and squirted her cat.

As soon as she did it, a lady came barreling out the front door. I knew it would happen. Don't ask me how, but grownups always know when the outside water is on.

The woman shook her finger at the little girl for a second. Then she snatched off the fireman's hat and went back inside. I could see the girl's hair now, wild and red and frizzy, almost bigger than she was. It was styled kind of like Bozo's.

The little girl stood alone in her front yard for a minute before sitting down on the curb. It wasn't long before she spotted our station wagon in the driveway. She was up and over to the car like a flash.

She cupped her hands and looked in every window. She didn't even check to see if anyone was watching. Then, before I had a chance to call my father, she climbed right onto the car roof and sat on the luggage rack. I couldn't believe it! We've had the car for three years, and I've never even been allowed on the hood!

"Dad!" I screamed at the top of my lungs. "There's somebody on our car! *Daaaaaad*!"

When he didn't come, I ran into the bathroom and grabbed him.

"Let's go! There's some kid crawling all over our car!"

By the time we got outside, the girl had opened

the tailgate and was sitting in Bill's empty dog cage. When she saw us coming, she grinned. Two of her front teeth were missing.

"Better get out of there, young lady," said my father, taking her by the arm. "That cage is for our dog."

The little girl clapped her hands. "Ooh! You guys have a dog? I *love* dogs! I have a cat. Her fur was on fire a minute ago, but I put it out."

My father and I just looked at each other. What do you say to something like that?

"I'm Molly Vera Thompson," the girl said. "I live across the street in the house with the nonny."

Dad and I looked at each other again. "Er, the nonny?" Dad asked finally.

"That's my grandmother," she informed us. "I call her my nonny."

Dad smiled. "Well, we're going to be your new neighbors, Molly Vera Thompson. I'm Mr. Jeeter and this is my son, Howard."

Molly's face dropped as she looked me over. It was pretty clear that she was disappointed.

"You mean you're *it*?" she asked at last. "You're the *new kid*? Pooey. I wanted one that looked like me."

For the third time, my father and I stared

blankly. Talking to this girl was like being in the Twilight Zone.

"You wanted a new kid that looked like you?" questioned Dad.

"Yup. You know, a little girl my same age in my same grade."

She paused for a second. "She doesn't have to have red hair, though," she added thoughtfully.

"How very fair of you," I grumbled.

"Oh well," she said, shrugging her shoulders, "it doesn't matter. You're better than nothing, at least. What's your name again, boy?"

Gritting my teeth, I muttered, "Howard Jeeter."

Suddenly Molly Vera Thompson's face broke into a big smile. "Hey! I got an idea, Howard Jeeper! Since you're a boy, we can play house and you can be the daddy!"

I'm not kidding. You could hear me groan all over Chester Pewe Street.

3

It was the next morning, but I still couldn't get the thought out of my head.

"*House!* She actually wanted me to play house!"

We had checked out of the motel and were on our way to meet the movers. I knew I was probably making too big a deal out of it. But *house* was just so insulting!

My mother shook her head. "Are we going to have to listen to this again, Howard? Now just cut it out, okay? Besides, like I told you last night, it wouldn't kill you to play."

"Yes, it would. It would kill me. I would die before I would be the daddy."

"I don't see what the big deal is," Mom continued. "You used to like to play house. Remember when you were seven and you carried Dad's toolbox wherever you went?"

I rolled my eyes. Couldn't she get anything right? "I wanted to *build* a house, Mother, not *play* it."

Mom thought it over a second, then smiled. "Okay then, what about that time a few weeks ago when you were pushing Gaylord in the carriage and you told little Harriet Miller that he was your son? What do you call that?"

"Lying! I call that lying!" I answered. "Harriet Miller will believe anything."

Just then my father turned the corner to Chester Pewe Street. I looked up just as Molly Vera Thompson was coming out of her house.

"Oh, no! Hide me! Hide me! Give me your coat!" I demanded, quickly getting on the car floor.

My mother peered over the back seat.

"Don't look at me!" I yelled. "If you look at me, she'll know I'm here!"

My mother continued to stare. "You're making a fool of yourself, Howard. Get up."

I should have known that's how she'd react. You can never count on your parents to hide you when you need it. It really makes me mad. What's the big deal about throwing a coat over your kid once in a while?

By this time my father had opened his door.

"Hullo! Hullo!" called Molly, running toward us.

Before I knew it, she was staring in our car windows again.

"Hey! What's that boy doing on the floor in there?" she yelled so the whole neighborhood could hear.

"He's hiding," replied my dad. My father's always a big help in situations like this.

When Dad got out of the car, Molly looked in the front seat.

"Hey! Mr. Jeeper! Is that your mother in there?"

"Our name is *Jeeter*," corrected my father. "And that's my *wife*."

"Hey! Is that a baby back there? No one said anything about a baby! Is that a baby, Mr. Jeeper?"

The trouble with Molly was that she never waited for anyone to answer one question before she asked another. I'd only known her a few minutes, but she was already getting on my nerves.

"Hey!" she called from the back of the car. "Here's that doggie you were tellin' me about. Is he tired, Mr. Jeeper? He looks kind of dead."

My father opened the tailgate.

"Pew," Molly said. "He's a smelly one, isn't he?"

My mother unstrapped Gaylord and reached in to pick him up. By this time I was off the floor. Molly peeked around my mother's back.

"Hi, boy," she said. "Is that your baby brother? I could baby-sit, you know."

My mother smiled. It was actually like she thought this little pain was cute or something.

"Have you ever baby-sat before?" Mom asked.

"No. But I know how. I can make him laugh. Wanna see? I'll throw him high up in the air and catch him. I saw a man do that to a baby in the grocery store once. My nonny said he shouldn't do that, but the baby was laughing. Wanna see?"

"Your nonny?" questioned my mother. "Oh, yes, that's your . . ."

"Grandmother," Molly chimed, finishing the sentence. "We live over there. I already explained it to your little boy and your father."

All of a sudden Molly looked up. "Hey! Here it comes!" she squealed, spotting the moving van coming down the street. Then she started jumping up and down like it was *her* stuff they were delivering. "It's coming! It's coming!"

While Molly was busy clapping at the truck, I stood on my tiptoes to reach my mother's ear. "Tell her to go home," I whispered.

Mom turned around sharply and frowned right into my face.

"Be nice," she ordered.

If you ask me, this is one of the stupidest things my mother does. She actually *orders* me to be a nice person.

My father greeted the truck and shook hands with the moving men. Then we all went into the house to show them where stuff went. When I say "we," I mean Molly too. She walked right in like she was part of the family or something. On the way she grabbed hold of my hand. I couldn't believe it! I practically had to pry her fingers off.

By the time we'd shown the guys around the house, Dad was acting like they were old friends. He kept calling them pal and buddy. I knew why he was doing it, of course. Before we left the motel, he said that if you act friendly, the movers are more careful with your stuff.

I wonder if my mother thinks that's "nice." I mean, I don't want all my stuff scratched up, but I don't think you should pretend to be friends when you're not. I think you should just be honest and say, "Hey! Be careful with that, okay?"

Anyway, at least they weren't the same moving men who had packed us up in Arizona. This time there were only two of them—Buzz and Ralph. They both had on orange overalls. Ralph was pretty thin, but Buzz weighed about three hundred pounds. Molly asked him if he was any relation to Santa.

Not only was the girl a pain, but she was nosy, too. She followed me around everywhere I went. "Do you have a piano?" she asked, looking out our living room window. "I love the sound of a piano."

"No," I snapped. "No piano."

"Oh. Could you get one, do you think?"

The thing is, I wasn't in a very good mood to begin with. Moving-in day wasn't much better than moving-out day had been. In fact, it was worse. At least on moving-out day, I had had Thornsberry and Roger to talk to. Talking to

Molly was like talking to the Smurfs.

Also, no matter where I sat, I was in the way.
Buzz and Ralph kept saying "beep-beep," as if they
were buses or something.

Finally, I grabbed my jacket and headed outside.
It was chilly, but it was better than Buzz's beeps.

Naturally, Molly followed. She sat down right
next to me on the porch steps.

"Honk-honk," barked Ralph. He was trying to
get by with the kitchen table.

"Hey! I got an idea!" offered Molly excitedly.
"Why don't we go over to my house and sit
there?"

It was like she hadn't even noticed that we
weren't becoming friends.

I shook my head and moved to the middle of
the yard. Molly sat next to me and tried to grab
my hand again. Then she wrinkled up her nose
and grinned.

"I like you, Howard Jeeper," she said. "Do you
like *me?*"

All of a sudden I just couldn't stand it anymore.
That happens sometimes. You're going along, trying to put up with something, then all of a sudden
it gets to you.

"Listen, I think you'd better go home now,

okay?" I blurted. "I think I heard your mother calling."

Molly got a funny look on her face. "No, you didn't."

"Yes, I did!" I insisted, holding my hand up to my ear. "Listen. Didn't you hear her?"

Looking puzzled, Molly stared at me a second. Then suddenly her face seemed to lose its happiness.

"I didn't hear my mommy calling," she said in a small little voice. "And you didn't either."

"I did too," I persisted. "I'm almost positive that I—"

"No, you didn't!" Molly yelled, interrupting me. "You didn't hear my mommy calling me because I don't have a mommy anymore! She and my daddy got divorced from me! I just live with my nonny now!"

I didn't know what to say.

"Oh," I replied, finally.

Neither one of us spoke for a while. Then Molly took a deep breath, like she had been doing some serious thinking.

"My mommy might come get me someday, you know. Or maybe my daddy will. . . ."

I was still feeling like a creep, so I just nodded. I

probably should have said, "Sure, they will," or something nice. But I didn't.

"Well," declared Molly, suddenly shaking her wild, frizzy hair all over the place. "I'm not going to think about that anymore. My nonny said I shouldn't worry my pretty little head about it."

"Okay," I replied stupidly.

After that the two of us just sat there watching Buzz and Ralph. Whenever Buzz picked up something heavy, he said, "Oooph!" and his face turned red. I guess being heavy doesn't necessarily make you strong.

Even though Molly seemed to be feeling better, I didn't have the heart to try and send her home again. She was still being a pain, but I tried not to be mad at her about it. I felt sorry for her, I guess.

Finally, across the street Molly's front door opened and her grandmother called her for lunch. I couldn't see her face too well, but she had on sneakers and jeans. Grandmothers don't dress the way they did in the olden days.

Molly jumped right up and started for home.

"Hey!" she shouted back to me when she was almost there. "Maybe I can come back later. What time do you take your nap?"

I couldn't believe she said that! Geez! Practically

the whole world must have heard her. A nap! I haven't taken a nap for years. I don't even like to *sit* on my bed during the day.

Of course, I didn't answer her. I just got up and ran inside. Ralph didn't see me and accidentally backed into me with a chair.

"Whoops! Beep-beep!" he said quickly.

It's a good thing Ralph's not a bus driver. By the time he'd honk, half the people in the street would be dead.

4

I waited until the movers left before I went up to my room. I guess I should have told them where I wanted my bed and stuff, but I didn't. What difference did it make? No matter where they put my furniture, it still wouldn't feel like my room.

To me what's really important is how a room *feels,* not where the bed is. Parents don't always understand stuff like this. To them the most important thing about a room is how it looks. Whether or not you've picked up your underwear,

stuff like that. But I wouldn't care if my underwear was stacked to the ceiling as long as my room
felt right. I want a room where I can go and shut
the door and feel like I've just closed out the
whole world, where I can cry into my pillow or
make faces at my mother.

The trouble was that my new room was so big,
when I closed the door it seemed like half the
world was still in there with me. My mother could
be lurking around and I could be making faces and
not even see her! My closet alone was practically
the size of my old bedroom. I know big closets are
supposed to be real great, but personally I like my
closets small. When your closet's too big, dead
guys with hatchets can hide in them. It doesn't
matter that you know dead guys with hatchets
aren't real. When you're awake at midnight, even
a pretend dead guy can be scary business.

Sometimes I have an overactive imagination.
It's hard to admit this, but even the bathtub in my
new house scared me. It was the old-fashioned
kind. Instead of looking like a normal bathtub, it
had four legs with claws on the bottom. The first
time I took a bath, I was practically positive the
tub took a step backward.

I didn't bother telling anyone. Why should I?

When you have an overactive imagination, no one believes anything you say, even if it's true. If King Kong reached in my window and squished me to death, my father would think I squished myself.

That night I hardly slept at all. I was scared to death. The more I thought about my closet, the more nervous I got. Not only could *one* dead guy live in a closet that big, a whole *bunch* of them could probably squeeze in there together. Take vampires, for instance—my closet could hold three to four coffins easily.

Also, it didn't help matters any that my windows didn't have curtains on them yet. I could look outside and see the tree perfectly. It didn't look like a tree, though. At night it looked like a huge ghost with twisted arms and bony knuckles. I figured it was probably waiting for me to go to sleep so it could reach inside and tickle me.

The other thing that drove me crazy was wondering where George Washington slept. My father might have been kidding, but it didn't make any difference. Even if old George never slept in my room, who knows how many other dead people did? I know they weren't dead when they were sleeping here, but they're dead now. What if they left something in the closet and came back to get it? What would I do if some dead colonist came back for his pillow or something?

When my mother got me up the next morning, I was still a little jumpy. My body felt tired, but my eyes were darting around all over the place.

"Well, you look alert this morning," said Mom cheerfully. "All ready for your big day?"

Big day? I thought. *What big day? Wasn't yesterday my big day?*

My mother started looking through the boxes of clothes still heaped in the middle of my floor.

"What do you want to wear today, Howard? Jeans okay?"

I grunted. What did I care what I wore? I didn't know anyone in Massachusetts. It's not like I was expecting a lot of visitors. As a matter of fact, I wouldn't have minded spending the day in my Porky Pig pajamas.

"Well, what's it going to be?" persisted Mom. "What do you think the other kids will be wearing?"

That's when everything clicked. She was sending me to school! It was the first day after the move, and she was actually sending me to school!

I should have known she'd pull a trick like that. I've got the kind of parents who think that if you miss a day of school, you automatically turn dumb. I can't even fake being sick. I have to prove it. I either have to have a fever or junk on my tonsils. If my nose fell off in the middle of the night and I didn't have a fever, I'd have to go to school and breathe through my mouth.

Anyway, after I found out I was going to school, I started feeling really sick. It wasn't like I was actually going to throw up or anything. This kind of sick made my mouth dry out, my stomach churn, and my skin sweat. Just the kind of stuff a new kid needs to make a good impression. . . .

I couldn't eat my oatmeal at breakfast. I've always thought oatmeal looks a little like slop, and my poor stomach just couldn't handle it.

As we drove to school my father kept whistling cheerfully, like we were the Seven Dwarfs going off to work. He went up to the classroom with me, but he wasn't much help. He said, "Hello, I'm Cliff Jeeter and this is Howard." Then he left. Thanks for the support, Dad.

My teacher's name was Mrs. Walton. She smiled at me and welcomed me to the school. I tried to smile back, but my mouth was so dry, my top lip got stuck on my gums. I must have looked like I was making faces at her.

She seemed nice, but I knew that didn't mean much. Teachers are always nice when you first meet them. Their true personalities don't come out until something goes wrong in the classroom, like when a fight breaks out during a spelling bee.

Anyway, Mrs. Walton talked to me for a few minutes. Mostly she just said a bunch of stuff about how "delighted" she was to have me in her class.

"Heh heh." I laughed nervously. I sounded like a real lunkhead.

Finally, she assigned me to a desk. It was just in time too. As I sat down the other kids started coming into the room.

I've thought about it a lot since then, and I've decided that the hardest thing about being a new kid is that everyone gawks at you. The way the class was staring at me, you might have thought they'd never seen dry gums before.

Why did it have to be that way? Would it have been such a big deal for them to have just said hi? I'm not asking for a welcoming speech—just "hi," that's all, and maybe somebody to show me to the bathroom.

Of course, by the time lunch hour came, no one seemed to notice me at all. It was like I suddenly disappeared. As we were walking to the cafeteria, two kids actually turned their heads away when I looked at them. I guess they thought I was going to try to eat with them or something.

When we got there, I was forced to ask a little kid from another class what to do.

"Hey," I said, tapping him on the shoulder. "Where do you get milk?"

"From a cow, stupid!" he yelled.

I glared at him for a second. I don't usually carry a grudge, but in his case I decided to make an exception. I'm going to wait until I get to be about two hundred pounds. Then I'm going to come back and stomp him into the playground.

Lunch was awful. I ended up sitting at a table all by myself with no milk. My mother had packed a sandwich and stuff, but I was too upset to enjoy it. Mostly it just tasted like lump.

The thing is, when you're eating by yourself, you keep thinking everyone's talking about why you don't have any friends. You look like a real loser, and you feel lonely as anything. It's funny. I used to think that lonely was something you felt when you couldn't find anyone to play with. It's not, though. Even in a lunchroom crowded with kids, you can feel lonely. Loneliness can strike anywhere—just like the stomach flu.

After I finished swallowing my lump, I wasn't sure what to do with my trash, so I just left it on the table. On my way out the cafeteria door, some man grabbed me by the back of my collar. He didn't say anything. He just spun me around and pointed at my trash.

I would have appreciated it if he'd have told me what I was supposed to do, but he just kept pointing. Finally I walked over and picked it up.

"I'm new," I explained nervously.

Without saying a word, he pointed to a big orange can with a smiley face painted on it.

"Oh," I said, meekly dropping my garbage inside. I had seen the can, but I wasn't sure if it was for trash. "Where I come from, garbage cans don't look that happy," I explained.

Recess was practically worse than lunch. I just sort of wandered around, trying to look like I fit in somewhere. I made a lot of trips to the water fountain. When you go to the water fountain a lot, it looks like you're playing hard and getting thirsty. You've got to be careful, though. After a few minutes your stomach starts to slosh.

I noticed that a bunch of guys from my class had grabbed a ball and were playing soccer across the field. It really made me homesick for Arizona. All I could think about was Roger and Thornsberry and the fun we'd had together on the soccer team. I wondered what the two of them were doing and if I would ever see them again. I wondered if they missed me as much as I missed them. As a matter of fact, I wondered about them so much that, after a while, I wondered if I was going to start to cry.

"Hi!"

The voice behind me sounded familiar, but I knew it wasn't meant for me. How could it be? I was a new kid. No one talks to new kids.

"Hi, I said!"

No one except Molly Vera Thompson, that is. Suddenly the voice was unmistakable.

I turned and looked down. "Oh, it's you," I muttered glumly.

It wasn't a very friendly greeting, but that's the kind of thing you say when you're depressed.

Molly wrinkled her nose cutely and smiled. She was holding hands with someone.

"This is my friend Sally!" she informed me cheerfully.

Sally looked scared. Like she thought I might hit her.

"What's wrong with her?" I grumbled.

Molly just giggled. "She's afraid of big kids. One stole her sandwich this morning. I told her *you* wouldn't, though. You're my new friend, Howard Jeeper."

"Jeeter," I corrected, beginning to feel annoyed.

"Jeeper!" Molly repeated cheerfully. "I like Jeeper better."

"It doesn't matter what you like better. You can't go around calling people the wrong name."

"Why?"

"Because it's wrong," I snapped.

"I know that," she retorted. "But I like Jeeper better anyway."

By now I was almost yelling. "Fine! Call me any stupid thing you want! But it's wrong!"

"I know that! You already told me that!"

Suddenly Sally started to cry. Then she sort of huddled over like she was going to get punched out.

"Trouble here?" bellowed a deep voice behind me.

Slowly I turned and looked up. It was the same teacher who had grabbed me in the cafeteria. Geez!

What was wrong with this guy, anyway? Who did he think he was . . . Rambo?

Quickly Molly grabbed my hand. "Nope. No trouble. I'm Molly Vera Thompson and this is my new friend, Howard Jeeper. Only I'm not supposed to call him that, only I like it better."

The man frowned and looked at Sally. "What's she crying for?"

Then the three of us just stood there for a second, watching Sally bawl. Molly shrugged. "Maybe she's crying because she had to eat hot lunch today."

Finally the man just sort of pointed his finger in my face and walked away. If you ask me, some teachers take playground duty too seriously.

As soon as he was gone, I pulled my hand away and put it in my pocket. "Look. Why don't you two just go swing, or something?"

Molly shook her head. "Nope. Can't," she announced. "I don't get to swing for a week. On Friday I pushed Frankie Boatwright off the swing, and now Teacher said I have to learn a lesson."

"Fine. Go seesaw, then," I retorted.

"Nope. Can't do that, either. I'm not sure what I did wrong there. All I know is, Teacher said I can't teeter-totter again until I can act like a lady."

By now I was feeling pretty frustrated. This was exactly what I needed—two little first-grade girls following me all over the playground.

"Look, I gotta go, okay? You two run along and do whatever it is you do."

Suddenly Molly's face grew serious. "You can't go anywhere, Howard. When you're at school you have to stay at school. If you try to go home, the principal will track you down with radar. Frankie Boatwright told me that."

Finally I just took off running. If I didn't, I was going to go crazy. I didn't even think about where I was headed; I just ran around the playground for a minute and then onto the soccer field.

Before I knew it, someone was passing the ball to me. I guess all my frustration had built up inside, because when I kicked the ball, I booted it so hard that it sailed right over the top of the net. It was probably the hardest I've ever kicked in my whole life. The bell rang then. But on my way back to class two kids came up to me and said, "Nice kick."

Maybe it doesn't seem like much, but those two words were the best things I'd heard in a long time.

5

When I got home from school that day, for the first time in weeks I forgot to be mad at my parents. I walked into the kitchen and, instead of being my normal obnoxious self, I started blurting out everything—all about being stared at, and eating lunch alone with no milk, and not putting my trash in the happy can, and Rambo. Then the next thing I knew, my mother was hugging me and my father was handing me a roll of Life Savers. I was sort of sniffling by then and Mom kept smoothing my hair and telling me

51

that things were going to get better. I didn't argue or say anything smart-alecky. I couldn't risk it. It was the first time all day I hadn't felt alone.

It was weird. Even Gaylord seemed to take my feelings seriously when I went in to see him after calming down. He didn't spit up on himself like he usually does.

"I don't know if I can go back there again, little fella, I really don't," I confessed quietly. "I was just so alone, you know? And I felt like such a loser."

Gaylord rolled from his back to his stomach. Maybe this sounds stupid, but it looked like he was getting into a better position to listen to me.

"It's not that anyone really tried to be mean to me on purpose, I don't think. Well, one kid did— the one I plan to stomp into the ground. But the rest of the kids just didn't seem to care one way or the other. It was like I was invisible or something, you know. I guess it's possible they didn't know what to say to me. But that's the trouble. I didn't know what to say either. So no one said anything, and I just sat around like a big lunkhead.

"You should have seen me at lunch," I went on. "I'm not kidding, Gaylord, I would have *paid* somebody—anybody—to eat with me. Well, almost anybody. I wouldn't have eaten with that Molly Vera Thompson. You wouldn't believe what she did to me on . . ."

"Hey! What're you talking to that little baby for?"

At first I thought I was hearing things. I wasn't, though. Molly was standing right in the living room doorway. She had actually come inside without even knocking!

Before I knew it, she bounded over next to me and was trying to tickle Gaylord's feet.

"Want me to change his diaper?" she asked eagerly. "I bet I know how."

I frowned. "It's not polite to just walk into people's houses."

Molly didn't answer. She was too busy trying to pick up Gaylord. I think she was trying to get him into position so she could throw him in the air.

My mother came to the rescue. She brought me in a plate of cookies and took Gaylord back out with her. The cookies were a nice idea, I thought. It reminded me of the TV commercial where this little kid has a hard day and his mother fixes him a bowl of tomato soup.

Molly stood over the cookie plate with her mouth all watery. If I didn't give her one, she would probably have drooled right on top of them.

I wanted to tell her to go home. What was wrong with her, anyway? I couldn't be her friend. The guys at school would think I was a wimp or something. They'd think I was like this kid at my old school, Ronald Dumont.

Ronald Dumont was a sixth-grader. At recess he played horses with the second-graders. He'd put a rope around his waist, and they'd pretend to steer him all over the playground. It was pretty embarrassing. He'd whinny and snort and shake his head like a wild stallion. Most of us stayed away from Ronald Dumont. Once you've seen a sixth-grader act like a horse, it's hard to pick him for your softball team.

Anyway, I knew that's what would happen if anyone thought I was hanging around with little kids. I'd get this reputation as a weirdo. And if you ask me, I had enough problems without adding that one to the list.

Quickly I turned on the television and tried to pretend that Molly wasn't there. Out of the corner of my eye, I saw her crawl into my father's favorite chair.

"Hey! What're we watchin'?"

Don't answer, I commanded myself. *Ignore her.*

Suddenly Molly giggled. Instinctively I knew she was wrinkling up her nose and smiling.

"This is fun! Isn't it, friend?" she squealed.

Once again I remained silent. I felt her eyes staring at me, but I didn't look. I just kept watching the TV like she wasn't there.

"You know what, Howard Jeeper? Your mouth looks grumpy. Do you need a nap? My nonny says when I need a nap, my mouth gets grumpy too. Do you need a—"

"No!" I blurted. "I don't take naps!" I couldn't help it. Why couldn't she stop being so stupid?

"Oh," she said, still staring. "Then why is your mouth grumpy?"

"It's not grumpy! I just don't like it here, okay?"

Molly's eyes opened wide with surprise. "Ohhhhh. So that's it. You don't like it here. Is it 'cause you miss your old house? I did. When I first came here, I missed my old house real bad. My mouth was grumpy practically all the time. It's not anymore, though. Look! See?"

I made the mistake of looking. She had her face ready for me. She was smiling so wide, you could almost see down her throat.

"Hey! Wait a minute, Howard Jeeper! I got an idea how to make you feel better!" She hopped down from the chair and bounded for the door. "Wait here! I'll be right back!"

That was it—she was gone just as quickly as she had appeared. It was like a miracle or something.

Wasting no time, I sprung up from the couch, locked the front door, and ran into the kitchen. Mom and Dad were unpacking the last of the boxes.

"Feeling better?" asked my mother. "Molly still in there?"

"Er, ah, no. She left. She might be back, though. So if you hear someone banging on the front door in a minute, don't answer it, okay?"

My mother stopped unpacking and sat me right down.

"Look, honey," she began. "I know Molly's a little hard for you to take. But I met her grandmother today, Howard. And I'm telling you, that poor little girl has been through a very rough year. Her parents split up and neither one seems to want her. She was in a foster home for a while before they released her to her grandmother. And then she had to come here on a plane from Ohio all by herself. She's beginning to adjust now, and her grandmother said that she hasn't stopped talking about her new friend, Howard Jeeper, since she met you. She really needs a friend, Howard. It won't kill you to be nice to her, will it? Think it over. Will it kill you?"

I waited until Mom's back was turned and nodded. How did she know? Maybe it would kill me. Maybe after what I'd been through, the strain of being nice could make my heart collapse or something.

Just then there was this mad pounding at the front door. It sounded like Molly was kicking the whole thing in with her foot.

"Hey! What's going on in there? Let me in!"

You could hear her shouting clear into the kitchen.

I sat back down on the couch while Mom hurried to the door. As soon as it was opened, Molly practically fell right inside.

"Whew! That was a close one!" she exclaimed.

Both her hands were behind her back as she bounded over to the couch.

For the next few seconds she stood in front of me, rocking back and forth on her toes with this stupid grin on her face.

"Guess what I got for you behind my back,

Howard Jeeper! Guess what!"

"A machine gun."

Molly giggled. "Nope! It's not a machine gun. It's . . . it's . . . it's . . . *Madeline!*"

Then, before I could stop her, she pulled out the stupidest doll I'd ever seen and sat it right on my lap.

Basically, Madeline looked like she had been through a war. Most of her hair was missing and she had red crayon all over her lips. Also, she was only wearing underpants and a wool scarf.

I got that doll off me as fast as I could. I just picked her right up and sat her on the cushion next to me. By now Molly was sitting in my father's big chair again, watching Madeline and me on the couch together. I can't remember when I've felt so foolish.

"There!" she said at last. "Do you feel better yet?"

I didn't get it. Why would I feel better?

"Isn't Madeline the bestest baby in the whole world? She makes you feel better when you're missing your old house and stuff. You can borrow her and she'll keep you company. You'll see."

Suddenly Molly stopped talking. And, just for a second, her smile disappeared.

"The lady at my foster home gave her to me," she added quietly.

It made me feel kind of sad. It really did.

All of a sudden, Bill trotted through the doorway. I guess it was what you'd call good timing. Molly's face lit right back up.

"Hey! There's that funny dog again!" she squealed as she scurried over to greet him. She threw her arms around his neck and let him sniff her. She sniffed him back and made a face.

"Hey! Is this smelly guy a watchdog? Does he protect you and stuff?"

I just shrugged.

"Madeline does. She's a watch doll. Madeline will protect you at night just like she protected me."

"Protect me from what?" I asked.

"Anything," she answered simply. "Like if you just sit her on your floor at night while you're sleeping, nothing will get you. Not even frog heads."

I wasn't sure I'd heard her right. Sometimes people say stupid stuff, but it's just because you didn't hear them right.

"Er, did you say frog heads?"

"Yup, frog heads. My nonny said they really

weren't under my bed. She shined a flashlight under there to show me, but the frog heads were hiding then. Frog heads don't come out till you're asleep. Then they open their big, wide mouths and wait until your fingers go over the side of your bed. Then they eat them."

The way that she said it made me sick. Having your fingers eaten off by frog heads makes being tickled by a tree sound like baby stuff.

Right after that Molly's grandmother called her home for dinner. I wanted her to take her stupid doll with her, but I didn't know how to ask. When someone's trying to do something nice, I've never figured out how to say "no thanks." My aunt Emily gave me some purple socks for my birthday, and I actually wrote her a thank-you note for them.

Anyway, that's why I let Madeline stay. It's not because I thought she could protect me or anything—I just didn't know how to send her back.

When I went to bed that night, I took Madeline to my room. I guess I figured that as long as she was spending the night, she might as well do it on my floor. I didn't expect her to watch out for me, though. I swear.

6

On my second day at school, believe it or not, I walked there with Molly Vera Thompson.

I was about halfway down the street when I first heard her.

"Hey! Hey, you! Howard Jeeper! Wait up! It's Molly Vera Thompson!"

I knew this was going to happen. I just knew it. But even though I had begged and begged for someone to drive me, both Mom and Dad had refused.

"One reason we bought this house was so that you could walk," my father informed me. "The exercise will be good for you."

"Hey, I said! Hold it!" she shouted again.

Two girls walking on the other side of the street started to laugh.

What was I supposed to do? If I didn't stop, she'd just keep shouting her head off. And if I ran, she'd run after me. Finally, I bent down, pretended to tie my shoe, and waited for her to catch up. The way I figured it, walking to school with a first-grader is bad enough, but being chased by one to school is even worse.

"That was close!" she yelled, running up behind me. "For a minute there I didn't think you heard me or something!"

Why was she still shouting? I was standing right next to her.

"Shhh!" I ordered. "Not so loud."

Molly's voice got quieter as she looked around us. "Why? Is someone listening?"

"Only the whole world."

Molly just shrugged her shoulders and fell into step as I started walking again. We had only gone a couple of yards when she wrinkled up her nose and started to giggle.

"This is fun, isn't it, Howard Jeeper?"

I started walking a little faster.

"Hey! How's the weather up there?" she called, looking up at me. Then she started laughing like it was the funniest thing anyone had ever said.

I didn't answer. What was I supposed to say? Cloudy, with a chance of rain?

"Hey!" she persisted. "What's wrong? Cat got your tongue this morning?" Her legs hurried faster and faster, trying to keep up with me. "That's what my nonny says to me sometimes. 'Cat got your tongue, young lady?' she'll say. It means that you're being quiet."

"Yeah, right," I responded. I wasn't paying attention, of course. All I wanted to do was get to school before anyone saw the two of us together.

"Hey! Why are we walking so fast? Are we in a hurry?"

"Nope," I answered simply. "I always walk this fast. That's why you probably shouldn't walk with me. It's probably not good for a little kid like you."

"No. It's okay," she replied, huffing and puffing beside me. "I like to walk fast. It kind of bobs you up and down, doesn't it? See how fast my legs are going?"

Suddenly I started to run. I just didn't want to be with her anymore, that's all. I knew she couldn't catch me. And since I was getting closer to the playground, I couldn't risk the embarrassment of what she might do when we got there.

This time Molly didn't even try to keep up. As soon as I started to sprint, she stopped to watch me go.

I didn't feel guilty, either. Maybe I should have, but I didn't. Only a few more yards and I would be across the street, heading toward the gate of the playground. Alone. I was just about ready to breathe a sigh of relief when I heard it.

Still on the sidewalk where I left her, Molly had cupped her hands around her mouth like a megaphone and was shouting in the loudest voice I ever heard: *"Hey, Howard Jeeper! Why're you running? Do you have to go to the potty?"*

I wanted to die. I didn't stop running until I got inside the building. I know the whole playground must have heard. I tried not to look at anyone's face as I ran, but I could hear people laughing, so I'm sure they heard. They probably even heard on playgrounds in Russia.

The bell hadn't rung yet when I got to my classroom, but there were already three kids sitting down. One of them was the girl who sits in front of me. She didn't say hi or anything, but as it turned out, she was the first one in my class to talk to me. After I sat down, she turned around and asked if I would mind getting my big feet off the back of her chair.

"They're not big," I answered.

It wasn't much of a conversation, but when you're desperate, you appreciate almost anything.

At lunch, I sat by myself again. Only this time I picked a seat next to the wall so I could sort of blend in with the bricks.

As I started to eat I realized that a lot of the guys in my class were sitting at the next table. And since I was blending in with the wall pretty good, I could watch them without being too obvious. The guy I watched the most was this kid named Pete. I guess I was sort of scouting him out to see what kind of friend he'd make. Scouting is what they do in professional sports. It's a sporty word for spying.

I thought Pete might be someone I could like. I had noticed him on the soccer field. He was pretty athletic, you could tell that. And he wasn't a ball hog. Pete was the kid who had passed me the ball right before I took my big shot.

The good thing about Pete was that when my kick didn't go in, he didn't start swearing or anything. When you get to be my age, swearing comes pretty easily, especially when someone blows a chance for a goal.

The other kid that I couldn't help noticing was this guy named Ollie. You could tell that he was the wise-guy type. He was real loud, and he talked a lot, and practically everything that came out of his mouth was a joke. He seemed like the kind of kid that grownups can't stand but kids sort of admire. The thing is, to be a wise guy in class takes guts. Kids admire guts. Adults don't. It's that simple.

When Ollie sat down, he took one look inside his lunch bag and held his nose. Then, without saying a word, he stood up and threw the whole thing into the garbage can. Back at the table, someone asked him what his mother had packed.

Ollie was still holding his nose. "Something dead and a cookie."

It really cracked me up. Something dead and a

cookie. I was sitting all by myself, but I laughed out loud.

After that some kid threw Ollie an orange to eat. Instead of peeling it, he put the whole thing right into his mouth. It must have hurt his mouth to stretch it that far, but that's the great thing about wise guys. When it comes to acting stupid, they know no limit.

Anyway, when Ollie was standing there with that orange in his mouth, even Pete cracked up. You could tell by the expression on his face that he thought Ollie was acting like an idiot, but he still thought it was funny. Even quiet guys like Pete enjoy a good idiot once in a while.

It might sound dumb, but after lunch I felt like I knew the guys in my class a little better. I guess that's why at recess I hung around the group that was getting ready to play soccer. I was sure somebody would pick me. Maybe they'd pick me last, but I'd get picked. It's sort of this unwritten rule every kid knows. If you're standing there to play, somebody's got to pick you, even if you stink.

Just like the day before, Pete and this kid Joe were the captains. Pete picked me before Joe did. I didn't get chosen first or anything; but I wasn't last, either. A kid with his ankle in a cast was last. Still, it felt good when Pete chose me. All of a sudden he just looked over at me and said, "I'll take the kid in the red jacket."

It's funny. I used to think that being called something like that would really bother me. Especially after Roger Grimsley had told me about that poor kid in the Kenneth shirt in his class. But the weird thing was, being called the kid in the red jacket hardly bothered me at all. Let's face it, after a couple of days of not being called anything, almost any name sounds good.

7

My father gave me some advice. He's tried this kind of thing before, but it's never worked out too well. The trouble is, most of the time his advice is about stuff he doesn't know how to do. Like during basketball season, he'll tell me how to shoot a lay-up. Then he'll shoot a lay-up and miss. It's hard to take advice like that.

"Horn in," he said one night at dinner. I was explaining how much I hated to eat lunch alone, and he looked right up from his pork chop and said, "Horn in."

"Er, horn in?" I repeated, confused. I guess it must be one of those old-time expressions they don't use much anymore.

"Sure. Be a little pushy. Stand up for yourself," he went on. "You can't wait for the whole world to beat a path to your door."

"Beat a path to my door?" I asked again. Another old-time expression, I think.

"That means you can't wait for everyone else to come to you, son," he explained. "Sometimes you've just got to take the bull by the horns."

"Oh geez. Not more horns," I groaned.

"Bull by the horns," repeated Dad. "Haven't you ever heard that before? It means you've got to get right in there and take charge. If you don't want to eat alone, then sit right down at the lunch table with the rest of them. Just walk up there tomorrow, put your lunch on the table, and say, 'Mind if I join you, fellas?' That's all there is to it."

I didn't say anything, but kids just don't go around talking like that. If a kid came up to a bunch of guys eating lunch and said, "Mind if I join you, fellas?" the whole table would fall on the floor laughing.

Still, I knew what Dad was getting at. I think it's something all new kids learn sooner or later. Even if you're the shy type, you have to get a little bold if you want to make any friends. You have to say hi and talk to people, even if it makes you nervous. Sometimes you even have to sit down at a lunch table without being invited. You don't have to say, "Mind if I join you, fellas?" though. I'm almost positive of that.

I have to admit that the "horning in" part worked out pretty well. The next day at lunch I took a deep breath, sat down at the table with the other guys, and started eating. That was that. No one seemed to mind, really. They hardly even stared.

After that it got easier. Once kids have seen you at their table, it's not as hard to accept you the next time. Then pretty soon they figure that you must belong, or you wouldn't be sitting there every day.

I'm not saying that after horning in I automatically started to love Rosemont, Massachusetts; or that I still didn't think about Thornsberry and Roger every single day. All I mean is, the more days that passed, the less I felt like an outsider. I guess you'd say stuff started feeling more familiar.

Like at school, if a stranger had asked me for directions, I could have steered him to all the water fountains and lavatories. For some reason, knowing your lavatories sort of gives you a feeling of belonging.

I guess moving to a new school is like anything else you hate. Even though you can't stand the thought of it, and you plan to hate it for the rest of your life, after you've been doing it for a while, you start getting used to it. And after you start getting used to it, you forget to hate it as much as you'd planned. I think it's called adjusting. I've given this some thought, and I've decided that adjusting is one of those things that you can't control that much. It's like learning to like girls. It sort of makes you nauseous to think about it, but you know it's going to happen.

By the end of the second week, most of the kids in my class knew my name. They didn't use it that much, but when the teacher said, "Yes, Howard?" they turned around and looked. So I know they knew.

There was still a big problem in my life, though. Very big. And you spelled it M-O-L-L-Y. She was coming over to "play" with me more and more. It was getting totally out of control.

I used to think that if you didn't want someone at your house, getting rid of them would be easy. You could just shout, "Go home!" and that would be that. It doesn't work that way in real life, though. The only time you can feel good about shouting "go home" is when you've had a big fight with someone or if you hate that person's guts.

That was the trouble with Molly. She was kind of a funny little kid, really, and her guts were getting harder to hate. And even if they weren't, my mother kept reminding me of all the mean divorce stuff that had happened to her. It was supposed to make me "think twice" about doing something mean to her.

Still, I found it hard letting her come over every day. After all, a guy has his reputation to think of. And like I said, once word spreads that you're hanging around with first-graders, it's hard to live it down.

I tried to talk to my mother about it, but the conversations were too short to do much good. Mostly she'd just find me hiding behind the couch while Molly was knocking, and she'd make me go to the door. "Stop being stupid and let Molly in," she'd snap.

Finally, one afternoon before Molly came over, I decided to just tell my mother the whole truth and get it over with. Maybe she'd yell and maybe she wouldn't, but something had to be done.

She was about to put Gaylord down for his nap when I stopped her in the hall.

"It's going to kill me," I announced.

"What's going to kill you?"

"Being friends with Molly. It's going to kill me. You asked me if it would kill me to be nice to her and the answer is yes. I'm sorry. But it will."

My mother held Gaylord with one hand and put the other hand sternly on her hip. "How?" she demanded sharply. "How will it kill you, Howard?"

I was prepared for her to ask this question. "The pressure. You don't know how much pressure I'm under as a new kid. I'm trying to make these great friends, and every day Molly's standing at my front door for the whole world to see. I practically have to yank her in the house so no one will notice. Don't you get it? Kids are beginning to know me now, and I just can't risk it."

"Risk it? Risk *what,* Howard?"

I took a deep breath. This wasn't going to be easy, but I had to try to make her understand.

"Risk being turned into another Ronald Dumont," I admitted reluctantly. "Ronald Dumont was this weirdo at my old school who didn't have any friends his own age, so he ended up playing with the little kids all the time. He whinnied, Mom. I'm not kidding. He actually went around playing horses and whinnying. And after a while all we did was make fun of him."

"Oh, for heaven's sake, Howard. You're not actually afraid that just because Molly comes over here once in a while, you're going to turn into another Ronald Du—"

"Yes, I am!" I interrupted. "Why don't you understand? I mean, I don't think I'm going to start whinnying or anything. But I *am* afraid that kids will think there's something wrong with me. They've already seen her walking to school with me. I'm practically positive. No one's said anything, but I know they've seen us together. The next thing you know, they'll start thinking that I don't fit in with them. Then pretty soon I won't. And before long I'll be out on the playground, tossing my head around like a wild stallion."

My mother stared at me for about ten minutes. Well, actually it was probably more like ten seconds. But the expression on her face made it seem a lot longer.

Finally she just shook her head disgustedly. "I can't believe you're serious. I can't believe you are so worried about what people will think that you can't be nice to a little girl who needs a friend. And what's more, I can't honestly believe that you think being nice to her will turn you into some kind of misfit. But I'm not going to argue with you about this anymore. I'm tired of it, Howard. I'm tired of you hiding behind the couch; and I'm tired of making you go to the door; and I'm tired of trying to make you understand how much she's been through. I'm not going to push her on you anymore, Howard. You do what you want about her. You handle it your own way. But just think about one thing: Someday *you* may need a friend. Not want one. *Need* one. And if you do, you'd better hope that you'll find someone who has a bigger heart than you do."

She didn't understand. I *knew* she wouldn't, and she didn't.

"Hey! Let me in!"

I rolled my eyes. Molly was kicking at the front door, hollering her usual greeting.

My mother stood there, waiting to see what I would do. I hate it when she watches me like that. It's like I'm on trial or something.

"I'll let her in, okay?" I said, annoyed. Then, without wasting any more time, I reached outside and yanked her in as quickly as I could.

My mother just sighed and walked away.

Molly's hands were spilling over with coloring books and crayons. She'd been coming over to color a lot lately. At first it really bothered me. But then I decided that letting a kid color at your house isn't really the same thing as being her friend. When the painters come and color my walls, I don't consider them my pals or anything.

Sometimes she wanted me to color with her. Usually I didn't. But once in a while I did a page. Just for the heck of it, you know. I'm not exactly too old to color, but almost. I guess you could say I'm right on the coloring border.

Molly really loved it, though. The funny thing was, most of the time she only used lavender and lime green. Even for skin, she'd color it either lavender or lime green. Once, when she was coloring a pig, I handed her this color called light pink. She didn't even look up from her book. "I only like lavender and lime green," she informed me.

"Yeah, I know. But pigs aren't lime green. You need different colors in your pictures to make them look *real*."

Molly stopped what she was doing and stared up at me. "It's just pretend, Howard. My nonny says pretend can be any color you want."

Then, for just a split second, she got another one of those sad expressions. "Besides," she added, "I don't always like real."

Sometimes I wondered how she did it. How did she go around acting so happy when there was all that hurt still inside her? Even I wasn't any good at stuff like that. And she was only six.

Anyway, as she sat there coloring, the telephone rang. I didn't bother to answer it. When you're a new kid, the telephone is never for you. I guess that's why when my mother shouted, "Howard! It's for you!" I felt sort of nervous and excited at the same time.

"For me?" I asked, jumping right up. "I hardly even know anyone here."

Molly thought it over for a second. "Maybe it's your teacher calling to tell you that she saw you bump Frankie Boatwright off the seesaw and you can't teeter-totter anymore."

I rolled my eyes. "I didn't bump Frankie Boatwright."

"I didn't either," replied Molly matter-of-factly. "He just wasn't holding on tight enough, that's all." Then she frowned. "It's not my fault he had slippery fingers."

"*Howard!* Are you going to get the phone or not?"

I hurried to my mother's bedroom and picked up the receiver.

"H-h-hello?"

"Hey, Howard. It's Ollie. Ollie Perkins. From school, you know?"

I was almost too happy to answer. A kid! A regular kid my own age calling me at home! Calling me by my name and everything! It was like a miracle!

"Er, yeah, hi, Ollie. What's up?" I managed to say, trying to sound casual.

I was so excited, I can't remember the rest of the conversation. All I know is that some of the kids were setting up a football game on Saturday, and Ollie asked me if I could make it.

Could I make it? Was he kidding? Of course I could make it! This was just the kind of break a new kid prays for.

"*Yeehaa!* A football game!" I shrieked as I hung up the phone. "Some guys are getting a football game together, and they want me to play!"

My mother ran into the room and ruffled my hair. "See? I told you things would get better, didn't I?"

"Me too!" Molly chimed in. "I told you that too! Remember, Howard Jeeper?"

"Yeah, I remember," I replied, still grinning. "You told me."

"Hey!" she said then. "When is it, anyway? I can come, right? I like football, I think. Yup, I'm pretty sure I do."

The grin left my face in a flash. I should have known this would happen. I never should have mentioned the game in front of her.

I looked hopelessly at my mother. Not much help there. She gave me one of those "Now what are you going to do?" expressions and left the room.

I think this was the part I was supposed to handle.

"Uh, listen, Molly. I'm going to tell you something. And you might not like hearing it, but I think it's for your own good. Okay?"

Molly closed her eyes like I was going to shoot her or something. I guess she was used to getting bad news by now, and she was trying to prepare herself.

"Okay, I'm ready," she said after a second.

"Well, it's not that bad," I began. "It's just that it might not be such a great idea for you to keep hanging around with big kids like me. You might end up getting hurt, you know. Take football, for instance. It's a really rough sport, Molly."

Molly looked positively relieved. "Oh, don't worry about that. I can just wear something soft and fluffy. Then it won't hurt if I fall down. I know! I can wear my snowsuit!"

Oh, geez. Her *snowsuit*. That's all I would need—I could just see me showing up for the big game, dragging Molly in her snowsuit.

"No! No snowsuit!" I blurted. "It wouldn't help. These guys are rough, and they'll tackle you and drag you around and kick and . . ."

"Hey! I got a better idea!" she interrupted. "I can be the cheerleader! I can bring my pom! I used to have two pom-poms. But I lost one, so now I only have a pom."

My face must have dropped right to the floor.

"Don't look so worried, Howard Jeeper," consoled Molly. "I can still do good with just one. I'll keep my other hand in my snowsuit. Here, I'll show you."

Then, before I could stop her, Molly hid one hand behind her back and started yelling the stupidest football cheer I've ever heard: *"Push everybody down! Push everybody down! Push everybody down!"*

I collapsed on the couch and buried my head in the pillows.

8

On Saturday morning I could hardly even eat my cereal. It might sound stupid, getting so excited about a football game, but I couldn't help it. I even talked to Gaylord about it after breakfast.

"I think this is the start of it, Gaylord," I began. "See, there are different stages you have to go through to make friends, and I think I'm in the last one. First you meet them; then you learn their names; and then you begin to say hi and stuff. I've been hanging around them at school for a while now. But the most important stage doesn't come until you start to do something with each other. Get it? That's where I am now. I'm in the *doing* stage."

Gaylord smiled. He'd been doing that a lot lately. I think he was really starting to admire me.

"Now, when Ollie and Pete come by to get me," I continued, "I'd really appreciate it if you wouldn't be in one of your crying moods, okay? Also, if they happen to see you, just smile and try not to spit up on yourself. They might think it runs in the family or something."

I wasn't worried about Molly. I hadn't told her the date of the football game, so I figured she'd still be running around in her nightgown or something, watching Saturday morning cartoons.

Also, Molly had been spending more time with her friend Sally lately. Several times that week I had seen them in her front yard, pretending they were cheerleaders. First they'd scream, "Hit 'em in the head! Hit 'em in the head!" Then they'd throw the pom up in the air. It was humiliating just to watch.

Anyway, a little after ten that morning, I heard

Ollie and Pete knock at the front door. They only lived a couple of blocks away, on the same street. I think that's why they hung around together. When you're next-door neighbors, you almost have to hang around together.

I was in my room, so my father let them in. I hoped he wasn't down there shaking their hands, but I knew he was. My father treats everyone like a man, even women and children.

When the guys came upstairs to my room, I was lying on my bed and pretending to read a comic book. I wanted to make it look like I wasn't really expecting them. I didn't jump right up either. I just sort of got up slowly, like this was no big deal.

After a few minutes, they started going around my room, looking at my stuff. This is a pretty tense time for a new kid, if you want to know the truth. A guy can tell a lot about you by looking at your stuff. Like if I was a real brain, I'd probably have a chemistry set and a microscope. Or if I was Ronald Dumont, I'd have a big poster of the Black Stallion.

But mostly what I have are games. You should see my closet. I have about thirty different kinds. They're not baby games either. Most all of them say "12 thru Adult" on the cover. Also, I've got about a million *Mad* magazines. *Mad* magazines make you look like a normal kid. I mean, even if a guy had a microscope and a butterfly collection, if he had a couple of *Mad* magazines floating around, you wouldn't be too worried.

Pete didn't check things out as much as Ollie. Ollie went into my closet and came out wearing my fuzzy slippers on his ears. You couldn't pay me to put somebody's stinky slippers on my ears. But that's the thing about wise guys—anything for a laugh. You've got to respect a guy like that. You just do.

Everything was going along pretty smoothly. We were kind of laughing and talking about stuff, nothing special, really. But at least I was starting to relax a little.

That's when I heard it. The front door. It was opening. I hadn't heard anyone knock, but I was sure it was opening.

I listened closer. Little feet . . . oh, no . . . it couldn't be! Little feet on the stairs coming up to my room!

Quickly I sprang up and darted for the door. It was! It was Molly! I could see the top of her frizzy red hair bouncing up the stairs. I couldn't believe it! My first big chance to start some new friendships, and she was going to blow it.

I shut the door just in time. I locked it. My heart was pounding like crazy as I strolled back over to the bed.

"Er, ah, listen, you guys," I said, trying to warn them. "You, ah, might hear a little noise outside my door in a second. But don't worry about it. If you just ignore—"

"Hey!" came the yell, interrupting me. "What's going on in there? Hey! Let me in!"

Pete and Ollie stopped what they were doing.

"Who's that?" Pete asked, looking puzzled.

"No one," I insisted. "It's no one important. Just this silly little kid from across the street. If we ignore her I'm sure she'll go away."

She didn't, though. She just stood outside the door and pounded harder. "Hey! Howard! It's us! It's Molly Vera Thompson and Madeline!"

Ollie couldn't stand it anymore. He hurried over and unlocked the door.

Molly plowed her way past him. It wasn't raining, but both she and Madeline were wearing black rubber boots.

I covered my face with my hands and peeked through the cracks. Sometimes life isn't as hard to take through the cracks. This wasn't one of those times, though. Pete was just sort of staring at her in disbelief. Ollie was already starting to snicker.

"Hey! Who are you?" she asked each one. "What's going on here? Is this a party?"

Ollie began to laugh out loud. "Hey, Howard. Is this a *friend* of yours?" he asked mockingly.

Molly stuck out her chest with pride. "I'm Molly Vera Thompson!" she informed him loudly. Geez, why did she have to be so loud? "And this is my best baby, Madeline!"

By this time Ollie was getting out of control. Every time Molly opened her mouth, he laughed harder and harder. The sad thing was, she laughed along with him. Little kids do stuff like that a lot. They laugh and they don't even know why.

Soon Molly was giggling so hard, she thought we were all having a good time. That's when she asked them to color.

"My nonny got me a new coloring book at the store yesterday! I can go get it if you want!"

Ollie fell right over on the floor. Pete just grinned.

"Well, we can't color today," he replied. "We've got to go play football."

Molly's eyes got wide as saucers. "Hey! You

mean today's the day? Hey, Howard! You musta forgot to tell me! Wait here! I'll go get my pom!"

Pete laughed at the sound of it. "Her *pom*?"

"Don't ask," I muttered, feeling sick.

Just then Ollie held out his hands. "Hey, Molly. Could I see your dolly for a second?"

You could tell he was up to something. You could just tell by the look in his eyes.

Happily Molly handed him her doll.

"Be careful with her boots. Okay, boy?" she asked nicely.

"Yeah, sure," he said slyly. "We'll be careful with her boots. Won't we, Howard? We just want to see if Madeline will make a good football."

Then, before I knew it, Ollie was sailing Madeline through the air in my direction. "Quick, Jeeter! Go out for a pass!"

I barely had time to catch her before she hit the floor. Her head twisted around, and both her boots fell off.

Molly looked shocked. "Hey! Don't do that, boy!"

Across the room Ollie held up his hands for me to throw her back. "Here you go, Jeeter! Right here!" he called.

As Molly hurried toward me to rescue Madeline,

I let her fly. I didn't even think about it. I just did it. That's all.

After that we started playing keep-away. I knew it was mean. Keep-away's always mean. But I did it anyway. As soon as Molly ran over to me, I'd throw the doll back to Ollie. Then she'd run to Ollie, and he'd fling Madeline back to me again.

Molly was getting frantic. "Stop it!" she demanded. "Stop throwing my baby. My nonny said you shouldn't throw your baby."

Ollie laughed. I laughed too. It wasn't funny, but I laughed anyway. After all, I didn't want to ruin Ollie's fun. He was my guest, wasn't he?

Besides, the whole thing was Molly's fault. Nobody invited her here. I *told* her if she hung around with big kids she'd get hurt. Maybe this would be a good lesson for her. Big kids and little kids don't mix. Her friend Sally knew it. Now maybe Molly would know it too. She didn't really need me like everybody said she did. She got along okay before I came, didn't she? She'd get over not having me. Little kids, well, they bounce right back. . . .

Finally Molly started to cry, sort of quietly. It was kind of pitiful, really.

Tough! I thought. *Tough. Tough. Tough.* She should have listened to me! Why didn't she listen to me?

Ollie tossed Madeline to Molly. "Here. Take your dumb doll. We were only having a little fun. We weren't going to hurt her."

For the first time that morning, Molly didn't say a word. Silently she gathered Madeline's boots off the floor. A second later she was gone.

Ollie made a cuckoo sign. "God. What a weird little kid! Where'd she come from? Mars?"

"Ohio," I informed him.

"Same thing," he replied, still grinning.

The whole time, Pete had been sitting at my desk. I hadn't had a chance to see if he was enjoying himself. I hoped he was, though. I hoped I hadn't done all that for nothing.

Suddenly Pete stood up. The look on his face took me completely by surprise. He hadn't been laughing, I could tell. Even his smile was gone.

He headed toward the door and then stopped, looking first at Ollie, then at me. He shook his head.

"You guys are jerks, you know it? You're really jerks."

After that he left. He just walked out my door and didn't look back.

The football game was awful. At least for me it was. All I could think about was that Pete had called me a jerk, and that I had to prove to him it wasn't true. I mean, he didn't even know me, and already he didn't like me. It was probably the shortest friendship in history.

Luckily, I got to be on his team. He didn't choose me or anything. The guys just sort of divided up evenly, and I went over to Pete's side.

We took turns playing quarterback. When my turn came, I handed the ball off to Pete every time. After my second turn at QB some of the other guys on my team started getting annoyed about it. Once, in the huddle, Aaron Felson said, "I got an idea, Howard. Why don't the rest of us go get a hot dog, and you can hand off to Pete."

That time I passed it to Aaron. Some guy tackled him from behind and knocked the wind out of him. Then this kid named Morty Harrelson came rushing over and started pounding on Aaron's heart to save his life. He said he saw how to do it on TV one time.

Aaron recovered pretty quickly and slugged Morty in the arm. I don't think you appreciate people pounding on your heart unless you're dead.

After that I went back to handing off to Pete again. It was probably real obvious that I was trying to get in good with him, but I didn't really care. All I cared about was getting in good with him.

Pete never thanked me for my hand-offs, but I was positive he appreciated what I was doing. He scored three touchdowns. How can you not appreciate someone who has set you up for three touchdowns?

When the game was over, Morty and Ollie and some of the other guys walked downtown to see a movie. Pete said he had to go home. I said the same thing. I didn't really have to go home, though. I just wanted to walk with Pete and try to patch things up some more.

I know this sounds stupid, but I was actually nervous about walking with him. I wanted to tell him how bad I felt about Molly and everything, but I didn't want to sound like a nerd. I was so desperate, I even started wishing my father was there to give me some advice on what to say. I'm sure it wouldn't have worked out, though. He would probably have told me to say something like, "I'm afraid you've gotten the wrong impression of me, fella." Then Pete would have fallen on the ground laughing, and that would have been that.

Anyway, mostly I tried to be myself and not to say anything too stupid. That isn't as simple as it sounds. Stupid stuff slips out of my mouth pretty easily.

By the time we reached my street I was more relaxed. Pete started laughing again about Morty pounding on Aaron's heart. I laughed real loud and hard. I think I might have overdone it, but I wanted to show him what a good time I was having.

Pete didn't stop walking when we got to my house. He slowed down a little, but he didn't stop.

"Well, I guess I'll see ya," I said, hoping things were better between us.

"Yeah. See ya," he replied, still walking away.

"Er, thanks for letting me play and everything," I said then.

This time Pete turned around and shrugged. "Yeah, sure."

I was halfway inside the door when I heard him

yell something else. "If we play again next week, I'll give you a call."

"Yeah. Okay, thanks," I called. Fortunately, I managed to keep from dancing around the porch.

When I went inside the house, I let out the biggest sigh of relief the world has ever heard. Proving you're not a jerk takes a lot of effort.

But even though I was relieved about the way things had gone with Pete, I still wasn't feeling that great. I decided to head for the nursery and talk to Gaylord. The kid was really beginning to come in handy. When I tiptoed into his room, it was dark and quiet. He was taking his afternoon nap. I sat down next to his crib. One of his arms was dangling through the bars. I didn't try to move it. I couldn't risk waking him up. When you wake up a baby from a nap, mothers go berserk. The last time that happened at our house, mine hit me over the head with a newspaper.

For the next few minutes, I just watched Gaylord snoozing away peacefully.

"Geez, it must be easy being a baby," I whispered. "Practically no problems at all . . .

"But just wait till you start growing up, little fella. Things get so complicated, you know?"

I thought about it for a second. "Too bad old Thornsberry isn't here. I bet he'd understand how hard this is. I could tell Thornsberry practically anything and he'd understand. He's a pretty sensitive guy."

I smiled at the thought of him. "I remember once, in third grade, the two of us went to see *Bambi* together. And when it got to the part where the hunter killed Bambi's mother, I started to laugh. It was really sad, though. Probably the saddest thing I'd ever seen. But, still, I started to laugh.

"Then I looked over at Thornsberry. He had this pocket pack of tissues on his lap and he was blowing his nose. And he didn't even care who saw him. He wasn't fake about stuff like that. All of a sudden I was real ashamed of myself for laughing, you know?

"I have a feeling Pete's sort of the same. He reminded me an awful lot of Thornsberry, the way he just stood up and said Ollie and I were jerks for the way we treated Molly. I mean, he didn't care if it wasn't a cool thing to do. He just did it."

Standing up, I rubbed Gaylord's back lightly and got ready to leave the room. "I bet if Molly lived across the street from one of them, none of this would have ever happened," I added regretfully. "They'd probably even get a big kick out of her or something. They'd probably have let her tag along to the football game and bring her stupid pom and not even have worried about whether anyone would think they were like Ronald Dumont."

I sighed. Poor old Ronald Dumont. Maybe it wasn't fair to accuse him of being such a jerk. Maybe he had just been misunderstood like me. It could be that when he pretended to graze on the playground during lunch, he was just clowning around. I doubt it, but maybe.

9

I was watching television when I saw them. I just looked up for a second and there they were—two little eyes peeking in the window at the top of the front door. I recognized them right away. They belonged to Madeline. Molly was lifting her up to the window to spy on me.

It had been three days since I'd seen Molly. She hadn't been back since the football game. I guess you could say we'd been avoiding each other.

After I saw the eyes, I got up off the couch and

cautiously looked out the door. By then Molly and Madeline had moved to the living room window. Molly was crouching down under the windowsill, holding Madeline just high enough to look inside.

It might sound stupid—having a doll spy on someone—but I didn't laugh. I knew it made great sense to Molly. And besides, the truth is, it made me sort of sad. Molly missed me. Even after what I had done to her.

Slowly I opened the front door and looked out. "Hi," I said quietly.

Still on her knees, Molly turned Madeline around to get a look at me. "Is it him?" she whispered loudly to her doll.

I guess Madeline must have said yes, because a second later Molly stood up and dusted off her knees. She didn't say hello. She just stood there and looked at me.

"Did you want something? Did you want to come in?" I asked.

She still didn't answer.

"Because if you want to come in, you can," I continued awkwardly. "I mean, you could watch TV or something, I guess."

She stood there a second thinking it over. Then she headed inside. It was really weird. She probably hadn't been this quiet in her entire life.

Once in the living room, she went straight for my father's easy chair. She seemed to feel comfortable there. Then she put Madeline on her lap, and the two of them started staring at me some more.

I'm not sure how long we sat there staring across the room at each other like that. It seemed like a few hours, but it was probably only a minute or two. Even so, it was really starting to get to me.

The thing is, I just didn't know what to say. I mean I know I could have said "I'm sorry." But I really didn't think "I'm sorry" would have covered this one. "I'm sorry" is a pretty lightweight apology, if you want to know the truth. It only handles little mistakes, you know? Like if you spill your milk, you can say "I'm sorry," and that's that. But if something really big goes wrong, "I'm sorry" almost sounds insulting. Like if you run over your neighbors' cat, you wouldn't just hand them the dead cat, say "I'm sorry," and go home. . . .

I think that's why we have jails. Jails are for the really big mistakes that "I'm sorry" just doesn't cover. Don't get me wrong. I didn't think I should go to jail for what I'd done. It wasn't *that* big. What I'd done was one of those things that was too big for "I'm sorry" but not big enough for jail.

I took a deep breath. "Er, ah, how is Madeline?" I said softly.

Molly turned her doll around and gently smoothed her hair. "You flew her," she replied in a quiet little voice. "You flew her all around the room."

The way she said it made me feel awful.

"Yeah, well, I'm sorry. I really am. Okay?"

She shook her head sternly. "Nope. Not okay."

"No. I didn't mean that it was *okay*. I just meant that I'm really sorry, that's all. I don't even know why I did it."

Molly continued smoothing Madeline's hair. "You did it, though. You did it and I don't know why either. Because I thought you liked Madeline and me. And that's why I let her be your watch doll. And that's why I came over to color all those times. And that's why I told my nonny you were my bestest neighborhood boy. Except for you're not anymore. And we don't care. Madeline and me don't care."

While she was talking her voice cracked, like

she was going to cry. I didn't go get her a tissue, though. I just sat there, listening to what she was saying.

"Molly," I interrupted, "it's not that I don't like you. I didn't mean to act the way I did the other day. I really didn't. It's just that the guys were there and stuff, and you know how guys are."

Molly glared at me suspiciously. "No, I don't. How are guys?"

"Well, you know, we just sort of stick together. Haven't you ever heard that old saying 'birds of a feather flock together'?"

This time she frowned. "What's birds got to do with this?"

"Nothing. It's just this old-time expression I heard my dad say once. It means that birds hang around with other birds. You know. Like if a bird was living in a tree, he would rather hang around with another bird than, say, a chipmunk or something."

I should have known better than to use an explanation like that. By the time I finished, Molly looked completely confused.

"What's wrong with chipmunks?" she retorted.

"Nothing's wrong with chipmunks," I said quickly. "I was only using them as an example to show you that people usually like to hang around with people like themselves. Like I'm a boy and you're a girl, so that makes us pretty different. Get it?"

After thinking it over for a second she looked up. "Okay. So do you or don't you like chipmunks?"

I felt like screaming. But instead, I tried to stay calm and to make everything as plain as I could.

"Look, Molly. Try to follow this, okay? I'm a boy and you're a girl. And boys and girls our ages don't usually hang around together that much. Boys usually like hanging around with boys; and girls usually like hanging around with girls. Does that make sense?"

This time she didn't think it over at all. "Not always, they don't. My uncle Russell's a boy and he likes to hang around with me. He even gave me the new boots I had on the day you flew Madeline. That's what I was coming over to show you. My new boots. Did you see how shiny they were? They looked like they had spit on them, but they didn't. They came that shiny."

I rolled my eyes. This was going to be tougher than I thought.

"Yeah, they were real shiny, Molly," I assured

her. "And that was real nice of your uncle Russell. But to get back to what I was saying, there's more to this problem than just me being a boy and you being a girl. It's our ages, too. I'm in fifth grade and you're only in first. That's a pretty big difference, don't you think?"

Instead of answering right away, she sat there for a few seconds. "I think my uncle Russell is thirty-seven or fifty," she said at last.

"It's not the same, Molly," I said, feeling exasperated. "I'm talking about kids. I mean, to be friends, kids should like to do the same stuff, don't you think? But you and I don't like the same things at all. You like to play house and cheerleader, and to seesaw. I like to play soccer and football. Do you see what I'm saying?"

This time Molly put her head down on the arm of the chair and covered it with her arms. She stayed like that for quite a while. And I had the terrible feeling that I had made her cry again.

"Molly, are you . . ."

"Shhh!" she demanded. "I'm thinking."

Then, without warning, her head popped back up. "Hey!" she squealed. "I got one! I thought of something we both like to do! We both like to color! Right? Is that enough? Is one thing enough for us to flock together?"

You should have seen her. Her whole face lit up. I'm not kidding. It was like being friends with me was the most important thing in her life. I didn't know what to say. So I just sat there, not saying anything.

"Howard Jeeper?" called Molly softly after a moment or two. Her face looked a little more serious now. "If you won't get divorced from me, I promise not to use the lavender crayon for my pig. I'll use 'light pink,' like you want me to, okay?"

Geez. I've never heard anything so pathetic in my whole life. Even when the hunter killed Bambi's mother, it wasn't as pathetic as this.

I didn't have any choice, you know? There was only one thing I could say, and I said it.

"I'm not going to get divorced from you, Molly."

The smile was back. But mostly what you could see on Molly's face was relief—the same kind of relief I felt when I found out Pete didn't hate me.

Slowly she got out of the chair and gathered Madeline in her arms. "Thanks, Howard Jeeper."

When she got to the door, she turned around and sort of giggled. "This will be fun, being friends again. Won't it?"

I nodded. "Yeah. Fun."

She turned the doorknob and stopped again. "Hey, Howard?"

"What, Molly?"

"Does this mean that we can play house sometimes?"

I rolled my eyes. "No, Molly."

"Oh."

As she left I laughed to myself. I guess I practically even got a kick out of her for a second.

Two days later she showed up at the front door with Sally. I really panicked. I mean, it's one thing to have one little kid hanging around; but I didn't want my house turning into a day-care center or anything.

When I opened the door, Molly was grinning from ear to ear. Sally was hiding behind her. I think the kid has a problem.

"Hi, Howard Jeeper!" greeted Molly cheerfully. "This is my friend Sally. Do you remember her? She's the one who's afraid of big kids."

I peered around Molly's back. "She's handling it beautifully," I said sarcastically.

"I know," Molly replied. "That's because she signed up for karate lessons. She already knows how to put on the little white suit they give you. She can bow, too. Bow for him, Sally."

Sally started bowing. She bowed about ten times before I could think of something to say.

"Er, nice bowing, Sally," I managed at last.

Sally bowed thank you.

"We just came over to tell you that I won't be playing with you today," Molly explained. "See, Sally's here to play with me, and we're probably going to play some of that stuff that I like but you don't. And I'd let you play anyway, except I don't think you'd have a good time and Sally said she didn't want you to."

I looked at Sally. She bowed.

"That's okay," I said, feeling relieved. "I don't need to play."

Molly thought it over. "Maybe you and I can play tomorrow or the next day. See, Sally," she said, turning to her friend, "Howard Jeeper and I flock together sometimes, except that there are other times when I play with just you, and he plays with these big, mean guys. Right, Howard?"

I rolled my eyes. "Yeah, right, Molly."

When you have a friend like Molly Vera Thompson, it's easier to agree with her than to try to explain. Even if it means agreeing with something stupid.

Molly continued. "And, anyway, we only like *some* of the same stuff, not all. Like we both like to color, don't we, Howard? Oh, yeah, and we both don't like chipmunks."

I just nodded.

I'm still not sure this friendship won't kill me. She's a funny little girl and I admit I kind of like her; but I still might end up dead.

10

Ollie called after school. He wanted to come over. He didn't even hint around about it or anything. He just said, "Hi. Can I come over?"

I stuttered for a second, then told him Gaylord was taking a nap. He wasn't. I just told Ollie that.

It's not that I hate Ollie or anything. But after a while guys like Ollie can start to get on your nerves. I mean, when you first meet them, they seem funny and everything. But let's face it, putting an orange in your mouth isn't really much to base a friendship on. Not when you've had the kind of friends that I have.

Besides, after I got to know him better, I found out that Ollie Perkins and I don't have that much in common when you get right down to it. He thinks a lot of stuff is cool that I don't. Like when he went to this big shopping mall last week, he got his ear pierced. A lot of the guys thought it made him look real neat. Mostly I just thought it made him look like my mother.

I still think he's funny sometimes. Like yesterday at lunch he got a grape stuck in his nose. He kept holding his ears and trying to blow it out, but it wouldn't come. Finally he had to go to the lavatory and stab it with a pencil. I'm still laughing over that one.

Anyway, besides finding out more about Ollie, I found out some other stuff about living here too. Take my street, for instance. Chester Pewe Street. I found out that Chester Pewe wasn't a revolutionary War hero at all. Chester Pewe was a crossing guard. Molly's grandmother told me. She's lived in this town all her life, so she knows practically everything there is to know about it.

"Sure, I know old Ches Pewe," she informed me one day as she was sweeping the sidewalk. "He crossed kids safely at our corner for almost twenty years. When he finally retired, they decided to rename the street in his honor."

I must admit the news was a letdown. I'm not saying there's anything wrong with being a crossing guard. But when you count on a guy to be a big Revolutionary War hero, finding out he stood on your corner with a stop sign is a little disappointing.

Even so, I couldn't let it keep me from writing to Roger and Thornsberry. Too much time had already passed. I still missed them a lot. And, besides, I wanted them to write back. I know this sounds stupid, but I just needed to know that they were still alive and everything.

Writing letters is hard for me. Usually I only do it if my mother makes me, like after Christmas, when I've gotten gifts from relatives. But at least when you write to a friend, you don't have to make up a bunch of lies. I mean, if a friend sent you a pair of purple socks, you could probably just send them back and say "no thanks." Especially a friend like Thornsberry, for instance.

Dear Thornsberry,

I'm not very good at writing letters. But I thought I'd give it a try. I wouldn't want you and Roger crying because you miss me so much (ha ha).

In case you're wondering how I'm doing, the answer is . . . okay, I guess. Things are really different here, though. For one thing, Massachusetts is a lot colder than Arizona. At recess you have to run around the playground in a heavy jacket and gloves. After you run, you get all sweaty on the inside, but you can't take your jacket off. If you do, your sweat freezes.

I haven't made that many friends yet. Mostly, there's just these two kids I walk home from school with. One sort of reminds me of you. (Not as ugly, though!) His name is Pete Jones and he's pretty quiet, so it's taken us a while to get to know each other. My mother says we're finally starting to grow on each other. (It makes us sound like fungus. Yuck.)

The other guy's name is Ollie Perkins. In some ways he's kind of a jerk. He can be pretty funny, though. He's always in trouble. Yesterday in school he didn't feel like doing his math, so he went to the nurse and said he had an earache. She sent him back with this big wad of cotton hanging out of his ear. He had to wear it all day. Pete and I laughed so hard, we couldn't even eat lunch.

There aren't very many kids living on my block. In fact, there's only one. Her name is Molly Vera Thompson and she's a first-grader. She was sort of a pain at first, but I've finally gotten used to her. Last night her grandmother had to go somewhere, so Molly ate dinner at our house. After we finished, she told my mother she was a better cook than Ronald McDonald. I'm not kidding. She says stuff like that all the time. You'd probably get a kick out of her or something.

Oh, yeah, I almost forgot. About the name of my street. Do me a favor and don't laugh. Chester Pewe was a crossing guard, but if anyone asks, I'd appreciate it if you'd say he was a Revolutionary War hero. Say that he hung around a lot with George Washington and the guy on the Quaker Oats box. It'll make it seem more real that way.

Well, gotta go. Say hi to Roger for me, okay? Oh, yeah, and one more thing. Remember that kid in the Kenneth shirt he told us about? The one who had just moved there? If you see him, tell him the kid in the red jacket says hello. I think maybe he'll understand. . . .

BARBARA PARK is one of today's funniest, most popular authors of books for young readers. She has written five previous novels, and children have consistently chosen them as their favorites. Among the many awards given by children that she has received are the Texas Bluebonnet Award, the Georgia Children's Book Award, the Milner Award, and the IRA/CBC Children's Choice Award.

Ms. Park holds a B.S. in Education from the University of Alabama and now lives in Phoenix, Arizona with her husband and their two sons.